W9-BRO-990

For Gabriella M.

Copyright © 1987 by David McKee.
First published in Great Britain by Andersen Press Ltd.
All rights reserved. No part of this book may be reproduced or utilized in any form or
by any means, electronic or mechanical, including photocopying, recording or by
any information storage and retrieval system, without permission in writing from the
Publisher. Inquiries should be addressed to Lothrop, Lee & Shepard Books, a division
of William Morrow & Company, Inc., 105 Madison Avenue, New York, New York
10016. Printed in Italy.

First U.S. Edition 1988   1 2 3 4 5 6 7 8 9 10

Library of Congress Cataloging in Publication Data
McKee, David.   Snow woman.
Summary: Two children with sex-role conscious parents debate whether to build a
snowman or a snow woman and decide on both, with surprising results. [1. Snowmen
—Fiction.   2. Sex role—Fiction]   I. Title. PZ7.M19448Sn   1988   [E]   87-16996
ISBN 0-688-07674-2   ISBN 0-688-07675-0 (lib. bdg.)

SNOW
WOMAN
David McKee

Lothrop, Lee & Shepard Books • **New York**

"We're going to build a snowman," said Rupert.

"You mean a snowperson," said his father.

"We're going to build a snowman," said Rupert.

"You mean a snowperson," said his mother.

"I'm going to build a snow woman," said Kate.

"That's a good girl," said her mother.

"Snow woman? Nobody builds a snow woman,"
said Rupert. "We'll build a snowman."

"You can build a snowman, I'm going to build
a snow woman," said Kate.

Side by side they built their snowpeople.

Later they ran indoors again.

"I need a hat and scarf for the snowman," said Rupert.

"You **mean** snowperson," said his father.

"Can I have some clothes for the snow woman?"
asked Kate.

"Certainly, dear," Kate's mother said, as she
went through the closet for snow woman clothes.

They put the clothes on the snowpeople.

Then their mother took their photograph.

At bedtime, Rupert said, "Will the snowman be there in the morning?"

"You mean snowperson," said his father.
"Yes, if it doesn't melt."

"Will the snow woman be there tomorrow?"
asked Kate.

"I expect so, dear," said her mother.

"They've gone," gasped Rupert next morning.
"So have the clothes, so they didn't melt," said Kate.

"I've **never** heard of a snowman walking away before,"
said Rupert.

"Probably because he never had a snow woman
before," said Kate. "Now what shall we do?"

"Let's build a snow bear," said Rupert.
"Man bear or lady bear?" asked Kate.

"Just a bear," said Rupert.